Denise Fleming

under

BEACH LANE BOOKS   New York London Toronto Sydney New Delhi

GROUND

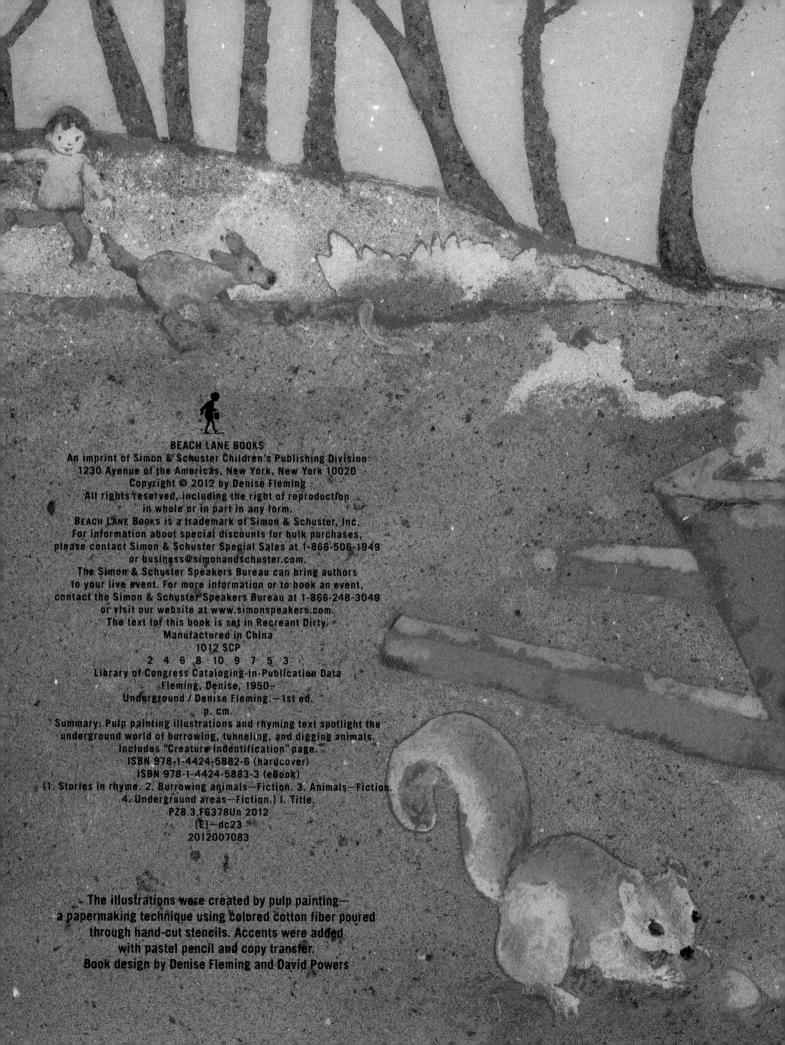

BEACH LANE BOOKS

An imprint of Simon & Schuster Children's Publishing Division
1230 Avenue of the Americas, New York, New York 10020
Copyright © 2012 by Denise Fleming
BEACH LANE BOOKS is a trademark of Simon & Schuster, Inc.
For information about special discounts for bulk purchases,
please contact Simon & Schuster Special Sales at 1-866-506-1949
or business@simonandschuster.com.
The Simon & Schuster Speakers Bureau can bring authors
to your live event. For more information or to book an event,
contact the Simon & Schuster Speakers Bureau at 1-866-248-3049
or visit our website at www.simonspeakers.com.
The text for this book is set in Recreant Dirty.
Manufactured in China
1012 SCP
2 4 6 8 10 9 7 5 3
Library of Congress Cataloging-in-Publication Data
Fleming, Denise, 1950–
Underground / Denise Fleming.—1st ed.
p. cm.
Summary: Pulp painting illustrations and rhyming text spotlight the
underground world of burrowing, tunneling, and digging animals.
Includes "Creature Indentification" page.
ISBN 978-1-4424-5882-6 (hardcover)
ISBN 978-1-4424-5883-3 (eBook)
[1. Stories in rhyme. 2. Burrowing animals—Fiction. 3. Animals—Fiction.
4. Underground areas—Fiction.] I. Title.
PZ8.3.F6378Un 2012
[E]—dc23
2012007083

The illustrations were created by pulp painting—
a papermaking technique using colored cotton fiber poured
through hand-cut stencils. Accents were added
with pastel pencil and copy transfer.
Book design by Denise Fleming and David Powers

For my sister,
Rochelle

Low down.

Way down.

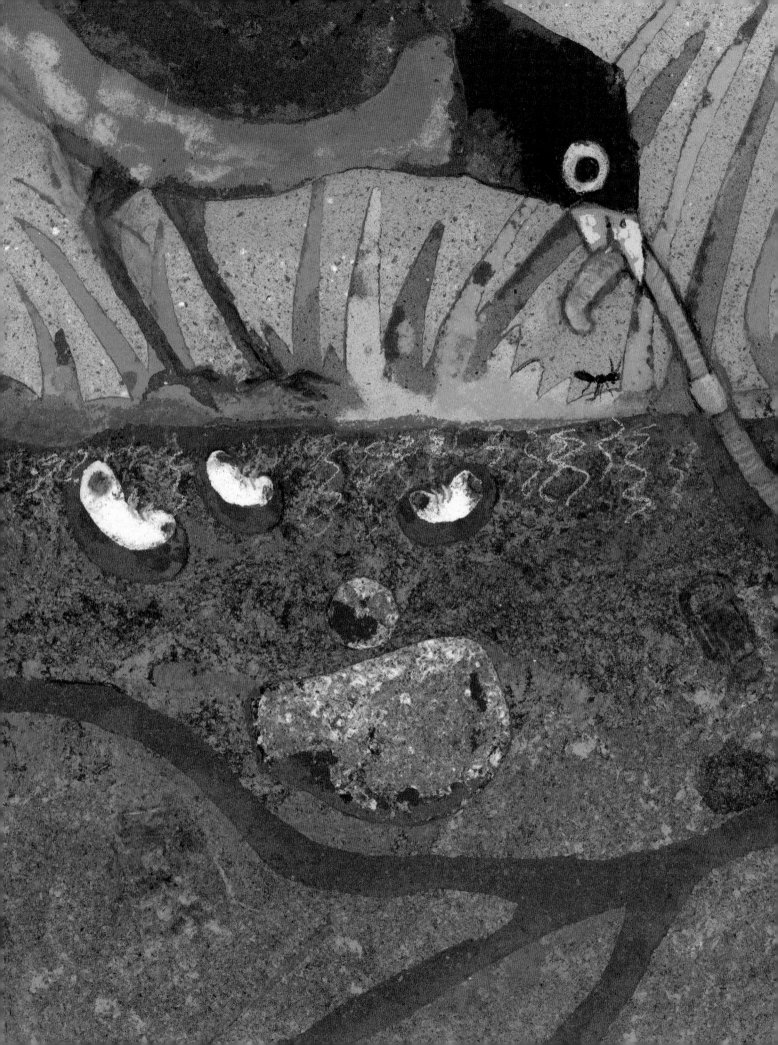

Under ground.

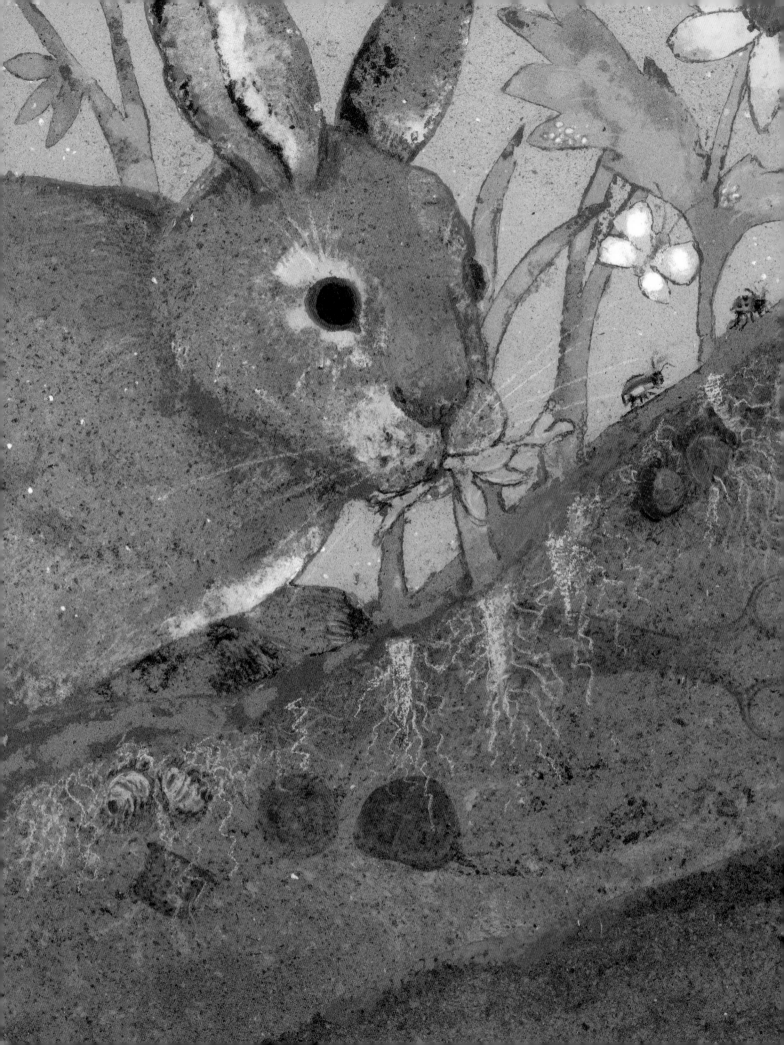

Creatures dig

and run around.

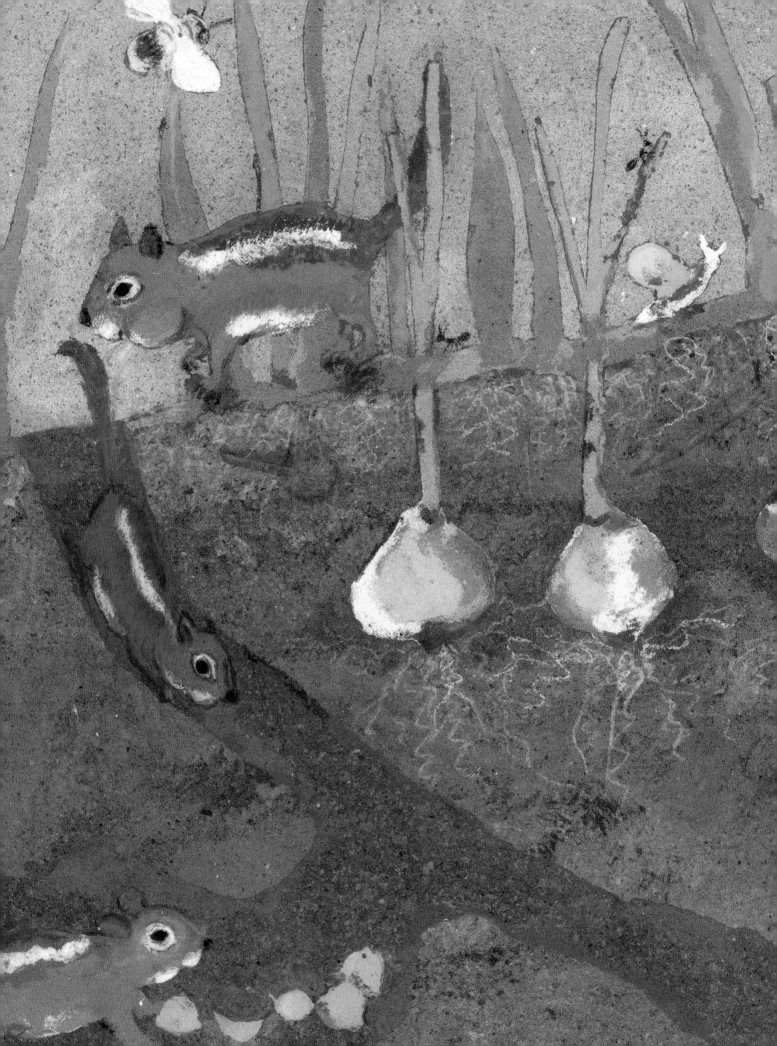

Past
highways
and byways.

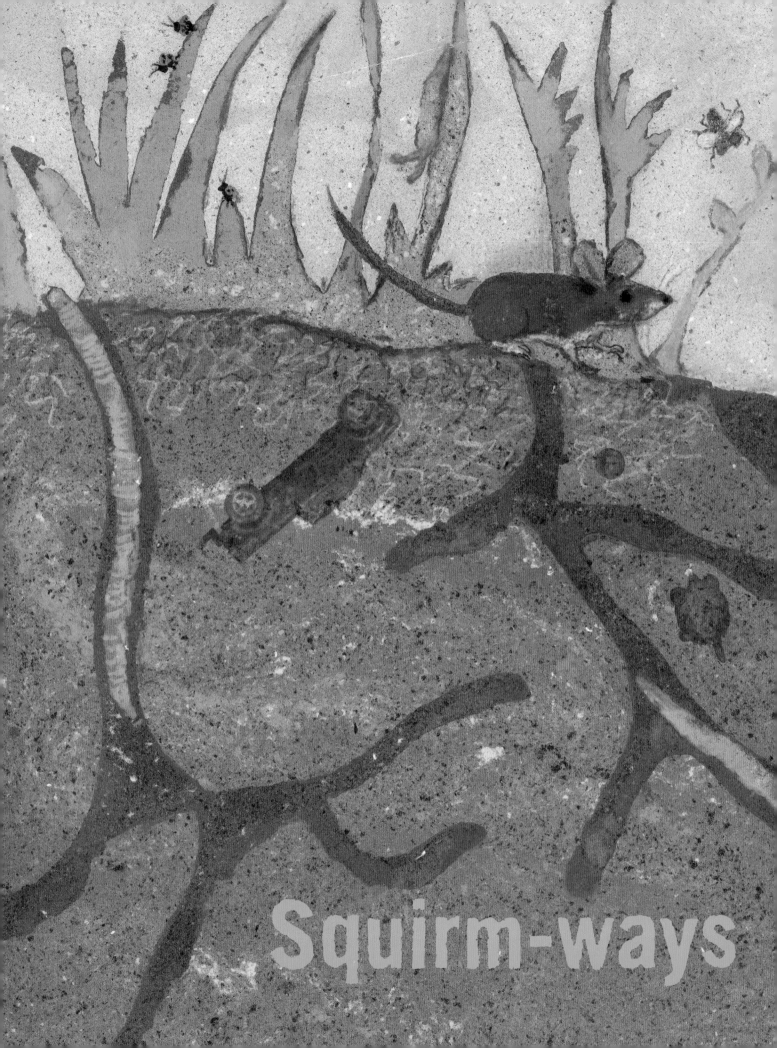

Squirm-ways

and worm-ways.

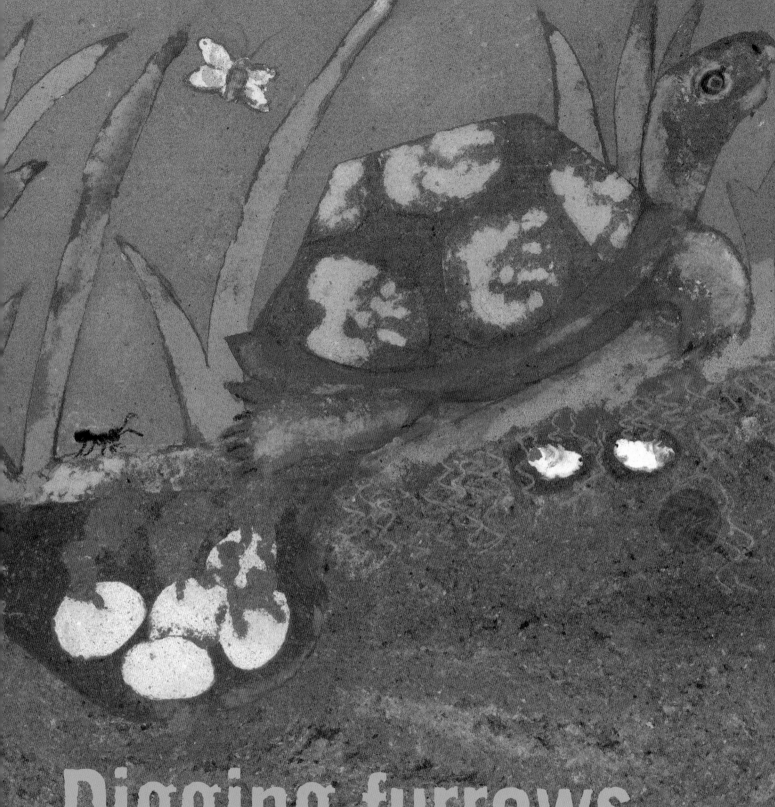

Digging furrows
and burrows,

'round roots

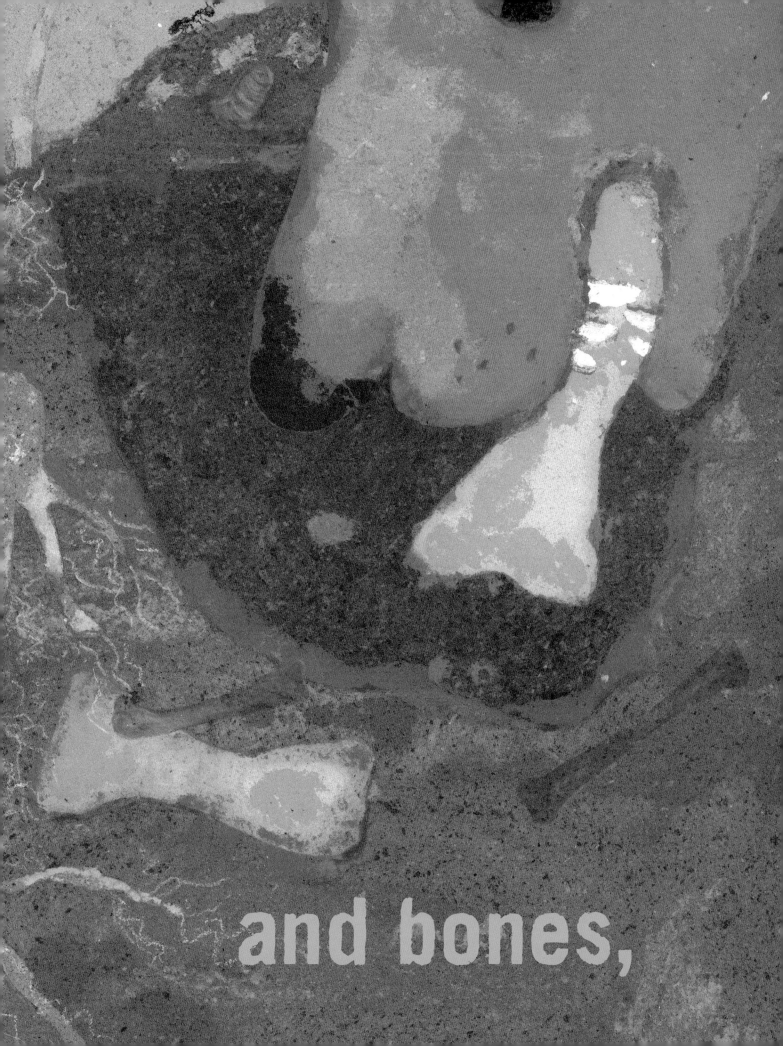

and bones,

rocks and stones.

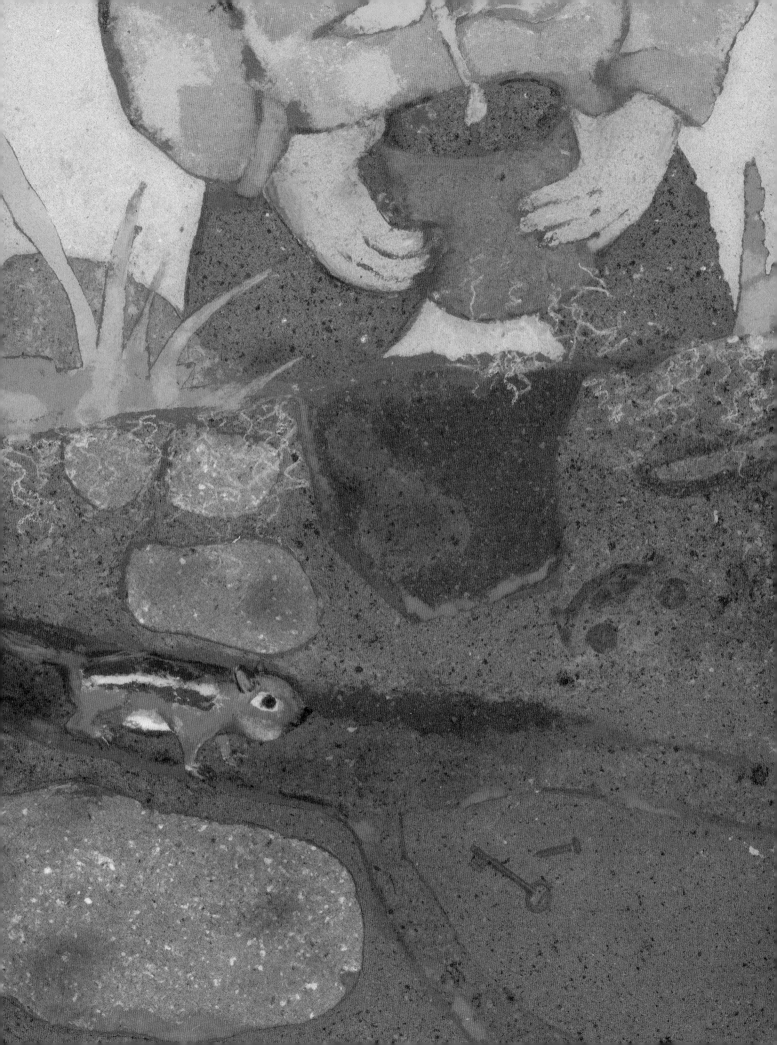

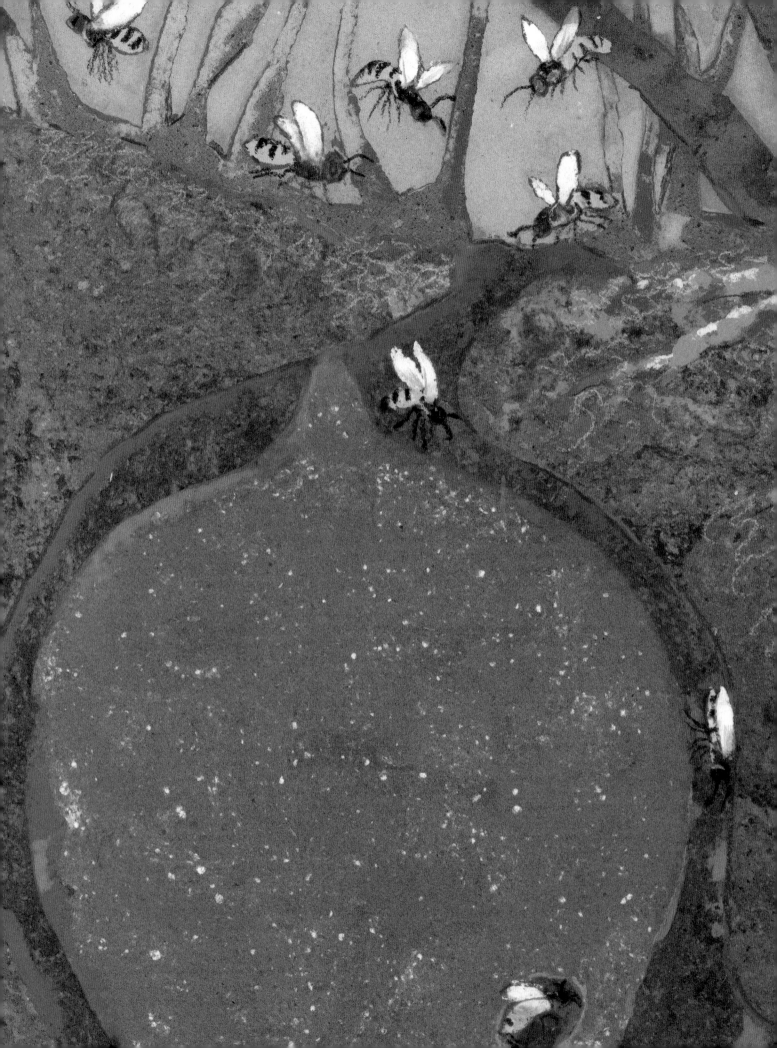

Funneling,
tunneling,

**working
their way
through
sand and clay.**

Low down.

Under ground.

Creature Identification

Squirrel—Squirrels save extra seeds and nuts by burying them in the ground. When food is scarce, squirrels locate their buried stash by using their excellent sense of smell.

Robin—In the warm months robins can often be seen in a tug-of-war with worms, a favorite food.

Grub—Grubs are the larvae of beetles. Some beetles lay their eggs underground. While underground, the eggs become larvae, the stage before the adult beetle.

Rabbit—Most rabbits in the US do not dig extensive underground burrows. They dig shallow holes or use other animals' abandoned burrows as nests for their young.

Mole—Moles have strong front legs with large nails for digging. They spend most of their lives underground in search of food such as earthworms. Their tunnels have nesting chambers and food storage chambers.

Cicada Nymph—Cicadas start their lives underground. They begin as eggs and evolve into nymphs. Some cicada species spend seventeen years underground before they emerge as a nymph. The emerging nymphs attach themselves to a tree or plant and shed their skin when they become adult cicadas.

Shrew—Many shrews raise their young in other animals' burrows.

Fox—Foxes will often enlarge empty woodchuck burrows to use as dens for their young.

Ant—Ants live in large underground communities. Their tunnels have chambers for eggs, larvae, and food storage.

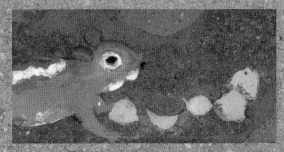

Chipmunk—Chipmunks are constantly foraging for food to store in their extensive underground tunnels, which include nesting chambers along with storage chambers and several exits.

Woodchuck—Woodchuck (groundhog) burrows are deep and have chambers for food storage and nests for offspring. The burrows also have escape exits. Woodchucks use their burrows year-round.

Deer Mouse—Deer mice dig burrows in the ground where they build grass nests.

Earthworm—Earthworms eat their way through the soil. The soil passes through the worm's body and the resulting waste enriches the soil. Earthworm tunnels aerate and loosen the earth.

Salamander—Salamanders burrow under logs or rocks where the soil is moist.

Toad—Toads often burrow in the damp soil under rocks.

Box turtle—Box turtles dig shallow burrows where they lay their eggs. They cover the eggs with soil for protection from predators. Box turtles also spend the cold months underground.

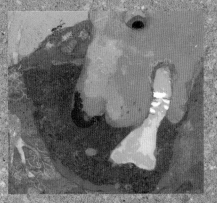

Dog—Some dogs are constant diggers. They bury their toys, bones, and food.

Garter Snake—Garter snakes do not lay eggs. They bear live young. Sometimes they will birth their young in empty burrows.

Yellow Jacket—Yellow jackets may build underground paper nests in holes they have dug or in abandoned burrows. They chew old wood and plant fiber to make the paper to build their nests. The opening to a nest burrow will appear as a small hole in the soil. If disturbed, yellow jackets become very angry.

Baby Rabbit—Mother rabbits line shallow holes with grass to make nests for their babies. They cover the holes with grass to protect the babies.

Trapdoor Spider—Trapdoor spiders dig tubelike tunnels and wait to snatch passing prey.